THE
SIDECAR
KINGS

THE
SIDECAR
KINGS

Jon Burcaw

Outskirts Press, Inc.
Denver, Colorado

The Sidecar Kings
All Rights Reserved.
Copyright © 2011 Jon Burcaw
V2.0

Outskirts Press, Inc.
http://www.outskirtspress.com

ISBN: 978-1-4327-7191-1

Library of Congress Control Number: 2011928966

Outskirts Press and the "OP" logo are trademarks belonging to Outskirts Press, Inc.

PRINTED IN THE UNITED STATES OF AMERICA

To my Mom,

the greatest MDA supporter there ever was.

Her spirit rides through every page.

"MDA camp week is the best week of the year!"

—MDA camper

THE
SIDECAR
KINGS

CHAPTER

1

A hazy, warm, July sun blazed over Valley MDA Camp early on a Wednesday morning. In these parts, a warm morning almost always goes hand in hand with drenching humidity. It was one of those days when a body felt drier in a bathing suit, submerged in a swimming pool, than anywhere else. The heat was the kind of heat that sent air conditioners to the brink of failure and made bad hair the rule, rather than the exception.

Cabin 22 was the coolest cabin in camp, regardless of how hot the weather was. Set at the end of a row of similar-looking 50's era bunkhouses, number 22 was shaded by a 25-foot tall spruce tree. It was the shade and the labored output of a desperate window air conditioner that kept the air cool inside, but this week the last cabin in the row housed five campers who had an air of cool that was uniquely their own.

They figured they needed a cool name that befit a cool cabin, so they got together on Day One of camp and made sure they had claimed a name fit for coolness. They ate, drank, and slept motorcycles. So they imagined everything they knew to be cool in a name and the Sidecar Kings gang came to be.

At age 12, Connor was the oldest of the bunch. He'd been confined to a powered wheelchair since he was three. Born with Spinal Muscular Atrophy Type II, Connor was learning to drive a powered wheelchair, when most kids were learning to run.

Close-cut red hair and full, freckle-covered cheeks made him the brunt of all the name callers' jokes. Carrot Top, Tomato Head, Freckle Face, he'd heard them all. The youngest of three children, Connor was used to getting teased by his older siblings at home. This year at camp, he couldn't wait to be the 'Top Dog' in his cabin, and be the one doing the teasing for a change.

Ten-year-old Eddie and 11-year-old Shawn both had Duchenne Muscular Dystrophy. Both walked when they were younger. Both now had wheelchairs for outdoor use and would eventually need them for indoor use as well. Eddie was tall and thin for his age, Shawn was short and heavyset. They were opposites in stature, but were good buddies at camp. These two guys had known each other prior to coming to camp. Even when the gang was together, these two were attached at the hip.

Ethan was nine. He shared symptoms of Becker Muscular Dystrophy, a more benign form of Duchenne. He still walked but tired easily. Ethan lived, it seemed, to get dirty. His face and, inevitably, the front of that day's shirt were perpetually marked by the most recent meal. He enjoyed the earth; playing in the dirt, sand, and mud, no matter the time of day or the season. He enjoyed the feel of these basic textures between his long, slender fingers. Nine fingernails were filled with dirt. The 10th, his right thumb, sported a very dirty, almost black bandage. Shaggy, blonde hair partially covered clear blue eyes that smiled on their own. Even though his physical challenges were gradually slowing him down, he still played in the dirt every chance he could get. Ethan also liked to make people laugh. Life was his stage.

Like Connor, eight-year-old TJ, the youngest and newest camper, had Spinal Muscular Atrophy Type II. TJ was an early wheelchair rider too. He came from a town a couple of hours drive from the camp and he had trouble separating from his mom and his sister on the first day of camp. He had not been away from them before. They were all the family he had. TJ's mom worked very hard at a local grocery store and when she wasn't home, TJ's 12-year-old sister, Rebecca, took wonderful care of him. She was TJ's arms and legs as he lived through each day. He couldn't imagine being away from her. But the camp counselors were experts at reducing the anxiety of the campers and their families as they parted for this very special week. On the first day of camp, when TJ had discovered the cabin he would be staying in was filled with motorcycle enthusiasts, it was much easier to say goodbye to mom and Becca.

Although similar physical challenges brought the boys to this place, at this time, it was the love of motorcycles in general and, motorcycle sidecars in particular, which was the glue that held this gang together, and set them apart.

All that mattered was the joy of the ride, a joy that went beyond all they knew. The talk of the previous evening was all about past sidecar rides the boys had taken. They talked until the wee hours of the morning. TJ did a lot of listening. A tow-headed blonde with a quick wit and infectious smile, TJ had a quiet intelligence about him.

Today would be TJ's first ride.

But today wasn't quite ready to start yet. Dreams of sidecar riding, boating, swimming, and game playing kept all the boys fast asleep, every boy except one.

A ray of sun worked its way through a cabin window and inside TJ's eyelids. A small voice echoed in the quiet cabin room. The hum of the hard-working air conditioner was the only other sound.

"Hey, Dave, can you roll me?"

Counselor Dave, quite used to being roused from a sound sleep by this command, squeezed the sleep from his eyes and looked over at TJ's tiny body.

"Sure, buddy. Be right there."

Dave was a local firefighter who took a week of his vacation time each year to be a camp counselor at Valley. He had been trained by MDA staffers to care for the kids. He, like many other volunteers, returned summer after summer to be with and to help the special campers that attended Valley MDA Camp. The kids at camp provided inspiration and life-long friendship.

His firefighting background made him uniquely prepared to handle the special needs of wheelchair-bound children. He embraced, rather than shied away from such challenges. Blessed with almost limitless patience, some said Dave knew something about life that made him unique. His eyes seemed to harbor a profound, unspoken story. The campers loved him.

TJ's disease made it impossible for him to do anything without help. He used a powered wheelchair to help him run. At home, with the help of his sister and mom, he used a machine at night to help him breathe, and he had a special pump to help him eat. During camp, he needed Dave to help roll him from one side to the other in his bed.

And right now, the sun was keeping TJ from returning

to sleep.

"Dave, are you awake? The sun's shining in my eyes. Can you roll me on my other side?"

Dave worked his way out of his own covers, yawned and replied with a smile, "Sure, pal, I'm up now and on my way."

Dave pulled the covers from TJ and gently rolled him from one side to the other. He positioned TJ's legs, arms, and head on the pillow just the way TJ had asked. During camp, Dave was TJ's arms and legs.

"Hey, Dave-what day is it?" TJ suddenly blurted out.

"Shhh, TJ! Keep it down-you'll wake the other boys!" whispered Dave. "It's Wednesday-you know what day it is! You guys were up talking about today until 2AM!"

"Wednesday," TJ echoed. "Sidecar ride day... Dave, I can't wait! My first sidecar ride will be today!"

"Hold on there, buddy! It's 6AM and you can't be ready to go yet. Get some shuteye so you can get ready to go.... later! Now go back to sleep!"

"Ok, Dave. I'll close my eyes, but I'm not gonna sleep."

Just as Dave had feared, the other campers in the cabin began stirring. "Boys, it's 6AM! You didn't get to sleep until 2AM. You HAVE to be tired!" Dave implored. "Please go back to sleep." While Dave knew sleep at camp was mostly hopeless, he wanted to make sure his guys got at least some rest.

"We are the Sidecar Kings," a sleepy Ethan declared from the other side of the room. "We don't need any stinking sleep."

Dave could barely contain a laughing outburst but managed to remain stern.

"Just one more hour, guys, please! I need my beauty sleep." Dave said.

"Ha, that would make you the sidecar queen!" Connor teased.

"Back to sleep, smart guy." Dave smiled and they all got resettled for a snooze.

After what seemed like just a few moments, Dave's alarm sounded. His radio was tuned to a local music station. As the radio came on, the announcer was reading the weather forecast.

"Your rock radio weather forecast is brought to you by Harley-Davidson motorcycles—ride to live, live to ride! It's gonna be another scorcher today in the Valley. It will be hazy, warm, and humid with afternoon highs in the mid 90's. Just like yesterday and just like through the rest of the summer, there's a chance of thunderstorms throughout the day. If a storm is headed your way, seek shelter, as the storms could contain heavy, drenching rain, gusty winds, hail, and frequent lightning. Now here's the new one from Jonny and the B's…."

Dave turned off the alarm and thought about the mutiny he would have on his hands if the boys would be stuck inside all afternoon. "Please, God, don't let it rain on these guys today," Dave said to himself.

TJ had stopped listening after he heard "ride to live, live to ride." His mind raced into the wind as he remembered all he had heard the night before.

After three more slaps on the snooze bar and near constant whispering in between in the cabin, Dave figured any more sleep would be fruitless, so he finally dragged himself out of bed and made for the bathroom to get his morning started.

CHAPTER

2

A few hours ride to the north, another kind of Sidecar Kings court was convening in the parking lot of Big's Harley-Davidson in Pleasantville. Big Bear, a giant of a man with a big heart and even bigger smile, sat in his office. Since he owned the place and his home was on the premises as well, he was always the first to show up for ride gatherings.

Big's shop was one of those places that drew people from all over. Big had nice bikes and great service, but it was the people, Big's family, his wife and kids, and the staff at the shop that made the business a destination.

He started the business back in '67 with his father and mother. At the time, Big and his dad, affectionately called 'Pappy,' by everyone, worked at a local factory making auto parts. Big worked first shift, Pappy worked second shift. When one was at the factory, the other worked at the motorcycle shop. Big's mom, known to all as 'Nana', was the only full-time employee back then. She worked at the shop all day while her husband and son continued working their day jobs, and took turns at the shop. The hard-working family began to see business increase steadily over the next few years and, in time, the men eventually quit their day jobs as the shop began to sustain them.

Bear married and later his wife joined them at the shop too. Two daughters followed later still. It was a real true family business that focused on others first. It is that simple notion that has made them one of the most successful businesses in the area.

There was one other thing that made this place different from all other businesses anywhere nearby. Every minute that wasn't used to sell or service motorcycles, was used to plan and take part in events intended to raise money for the MDA. The business was the family and the family was the business.

That's why today was one of Bear's favorite days of the summer. He was about to take part in two of the things he loved the most, ride motorcycles with his friends and give MDA campers rides. He had been arranging these rides for the last 20 years. One visit to a camp all those years ago was all it took for the family to get hooked.

As he sipped his morning coffee, he pulled a very timeworn, curled slip of paper from his shirt pocket and read through the list of riders' names who usually rode this ride.

Bear smiled as he read through the names. For most riders, he had written down only the nicknames. To anyone else, the list was just a group of unlikely words. But to him, each name was a story. Some of the stories brief, others quite colorful. Some of the names were as old as the curled up piece of paper they were written on. As he read through them for the thousandth time, he could hear his friends' bikes coming into the parking lot. Bear kept the list, not so much to remember who was riding, but as a reminder of how lucky he was to have such great friends.

Goose

Stretch & Mel

John Deere

Seven

Spud

Smiley

Froggy

Arizona Mike

Pop Pop Jack

Lil Load

Load.

Goose- an auto mechanic by trade, was riding through a nearby town one day when a flock of geese decided to cross the road in front of him. After his bike was stopped, he honked the horn to get the geese moving. No one is quite sure what happened next. The geese either tried to make him their leader or they attacked. The local police had to be summoned to clear the road. Goose was ticketed for disturbing the peace and became forever known as "Gooseman." To make sure it stuck, Goose had his name tattooed on his left shoulder, just above three geese flying in formation. He would be bringing a sidecar rig with him. While he enjoyed all group rides, he especially enjoyed this one because of how much it meant to the kids at the camp.

John Deere- or JD for short, earned his name when he was riding with a group of other riders on a country road that meandered through a corn field. The road the group was riding on turned, but JD apparently was paying attention to something else and he went straight into the corn. He rode through the corn until he reached a field access road and returned to his friends a short time later, fortunately unharmed. One of the riders commented on his bike CB radio, "Hey, he looks like a John Deere tractor coming out of there!" And another nickname was born. With snow-white hair and beard, JD could pass for a thin Santa Claus, the one that hadn't eaten enough for Christmas yet. A self-employed wood furniture maker, JD turned hardwood lumber into beautiful, long-lasting chairs, tables, and beds. He had been on all the rides. The first one changed him, just like it did for Bear and his family, and JD returned for the ride every year since. He, too, would be bringing a hack, a sidecar rig, along with him. His machine was special. It was built especially for giving disabled children rides. With its sleek, jet black fighter cockpit styling, his machine turned many heads while riding down the road.

Spud Muffin, or Spud for short, was sitting in a restaurant with friends when he ordered French fries and pierogies with his order. The riders who were with him noted his double order of potatoes and then hung the nickname on him. Spud was a manager for a small custom circuit board shop. Sporting slicked back black hair, a goatee, and piercing blue eyes, Spud was never far from a laugh. He brought a two-wheeler on this ride.

Froggy was a little simpler. His real name was Kermit. He had to be called Froggy. With shoulder-length white hair and a very lengthy beard, sometimes held in check by rubber bands, Froggy could light up the day with his smile. His rig was green, with black spots added for comical good measure. The word 'RIB-BIT' was inscribed on his personalized license plate. He rode his nickname to its logical extreme.

PopPop Jack was a grandfather and that's what his

grandkids called him. And then so did everyone else. Jack had taken part in the ride the last couple of years. He enjoyed the riding as much as being with the kids. He particularly enjoyed helping the campers into the sidecars. Jack's grandson had been a camper, so he knew about the life of a child in a wheelchair better than most riders. Jack was a retired foundry manager who liked to cut grass and he liked to build and fix things. He was truly a "Jack of all trades!" Jack was on two wheels this morning.

Stretch was close to 7 feet tall, his height conjured his nickname. His wife, Mel, was just a dash under 5 feet tall. They were easy to spot because of the huge difference in height. And they were always together in their purple sidecar rig. A retired utility lineman, Stretch loved to take pictures. He had huge collections of pictures from previous rides. He believed every camper should have a picture of themselves to remember this special day. Armed with all kinds of photographic equipment, he would be the event photographer for the day.

Mel was a retired school nurse who had great patience for all children. She was also an excellent cook. Whenever Big's family put on a fund-raising event at the shop, Mel was always cooking and serving something to the patrons. She and Stretch always selflessly gave their time.

Seven was a shop employee and a motorcycle drag racer. The number was emblazoned on his racing bike. And it became his nickname. Even though he took part in a noisy, violently fast sport, Seven was the quietest of all the riders. While he never really mentioned why he decided to do this ride, it was clear he enjoyed being with his friends and the kids as well. Seven preferred two wheels, to three.

Smiley loved to ride and riding made him smile. Whether it was sunny, raining, or freezing cold, this rider smiled through it all. One rainy October day a few years back, Smiley decided to visit his brother who lived over 500 miles away. Most riders would have postponed or canceled the trip because of the very poor weather conditions that day, but he decided to go in the face of the storm and rode through 10 hours of downpours to put a smile on his brother's face, on his 40th birthday. Afterward, he had learned that two tropical storms came together over the region he was riding through that miserable day. He realized then how lucky he was to have remained upright for the entire trip.

Arizona Mike wanted everyone to know where he was from, so his home state was also his name. He was a long-haul truck driver and frequently traveled back and forth across the country. Mike enjoyed telling stories. He particularly enjoyed embellishing the truth, stretching it sometimes to questionable extremes. One of his questionable stories involved the time when a black bear had somehow worked its way into a trailer filled with chocolate bars he was hauling. He claimed he was sleeping in the sleeper cab of the truck, parked in a rest area along a remote part of an interstate highway. He awoke to the sounds of what he thought was someone with a bad bellyache. He cautiously left his rig with his trusty baseball bat for protection. He said he walked to the back of the trailer and discovered the bear lying in a big pile of partially eaten chocolate bars. The bear appeared to be holding its stomach, Mike said. One of the rear trailer doors was open and the chocolate bar boxes the bear was able to remove from the back of the trailer were all over the ground. The bear was lying amidst the pile. Mike claimed he had frightened the bear away, but not before several hundred pounds of chocolate had disappeared. The

Photo by Jon Burcaw

only part of the story that anyone could verify was that there was missing chocolate. He never did say how the bear was able to open the locked trailer door. Mike stopped hauling chocolate after that run. Unlike chocolate, his sidecar rig was a sparkling pearly white color.

The story of Load and Li'l Load was known only to Bear and these two riders. Bear also had another nickname. He was also known as Big Load. These names came back with the guys after they rode together through the Mojave Desert. Each of these three had their own version of how the names were bestowed. Nobody but the three Loads know the true origin of these names. And they like it that way.

Bear's daughters, Cherie and Denise, were expert riders and would be riding the remaining hacks on the ride today.

In all, 20 riders met to get ready for the ride. Men and women from all walks of life got together to share a common interest. They all rode Harley–Davidsons, they all loved to ride, and today they couldn't wait to get to their destination.

There were seven sidecar rigs making the run. These bikes were special. There was magic in each one. Whenever anyone rode in a sidecar, two things happened. They didn't want to stop riding when the ride was over and they all had crazy smiles that just stuck. There was no other experience like it in the world.

Of the seven rigs, six of them were similar, only

differing in color. The seventh sidecar was JD's Road King. The top half of the fiberglass nose was on a hinge and that made it easy for anyone to get in and out. Today that would come in real handy.

The seven sidecar rigs were accompanied by 10 more bikes along for the ride. These two-wheeled riders went along to help get the kids in and out of the sidecars. They also helped to increase the 'cool' factor. More bikes meant a bigger, louder bang on arrival.

The riders were excited to get on the road and begin a very special day of riding. Before they left, there was a rider's meeting, the time when they all got together and talked about safety. Big Bear had come out of his office and asked Goose to whistle as loudly as he could to get everyone's attention. Goose could whistle as loud as anyone.

Goose puckered his lips and let rip a shrill conversation-stopping wail. Jack wasn't prepared for the volume of the whistle and he dropped his helmet attempting to cover his ears.

"Yo, Goosey!!! Send up a little warning the next time ya do that!"

"Hey, Jack, sorry about that! Gotta admit, though—it was pretty funny to watch you jump!"

After some laughter, Bear took over.

"Awright!" Bear said. "Listen up! The sidecars will settle

in behind me and JD. The rest of you fall in behind them."
Big Bear was a longtime rider and the group always knew to
listen to him. "Now I don't wanna scare ya, but it's a pretty
good bet we're gonna hit some rain before we're done. If you
don't wanna ride wet, either leave now or have your rain gear
handy."

He paused to see if anyone was going to chicken out.
Just like every other time, nobody did. "Ok, then. Let's
mount up and have some fun!"

Helmets were cinched down tight, starter buttons
were stabbed and quickly each bike roared to life. The
unmistakable rumble of a gang of Harleys filled the country
air. The string of bikes hung there for a moment to take in
the sight and sound. Then off they went down the road in a
flourish of rolling thunder.

No one could have imagined how adventurous this trip
was going to get.

CHAPTER

3

All the boys finally got situated in their chairs and prepared to start the day. Tuesday had been Tie-dye T-shirt Day and the boys all made similar shirts with the words Sidecar Kings emblazoned across the front. Today, it was a club rule- everyone in the gang wore the Kings T-shirts. They all looked like they had been made the same way, except for Ethan's. He had a mishap with some green dye and ended up getting more dye on himself than his shirt. Dave smiled at Ethan's still-green hands.

"Ethan, you gonna eat breakfast with those green hands? Let me change that bandage. That looks disgusting."

"Aw, Dave. Ya sound like my mom!" Ethan replied. "I want to try to set a world record for wearing a bandage on my thumb the longest."

"Good luck with that, kid. I thought the shirts were gonna be orange and black," Dave said. "How come your shirt and hands are green?"

"Because I thought the green dye was black," Ethan responded sheepishly. "Somebody musta changed the colors before I dipped my shirt."

"Who dipped before you?" Dave asked.

"We all sorta dipped at the same time. I'm tellin' ya, the color got changed."

Connor, Eddie, and Shawn giggled over on the other side of the room. Dave glared at them and instantly knew Ethan had been punked by the boys.

"No worries, E-man," Dave reassured. "You guys all have the Sidecar King logo you came up with. You look cooler than cool, no matter the color."

For Ethan, that's all that mattered.

As the boys got ready to leave for breakfast, Dave had to get a picture of the gang as they looked right then. Sometimes, some moments need to be frozen. This was one. Just like a real club, these kids all had stories to tell. Today at this moment, this picture would tell a thousand-word story.

The boys all huddled together as close as their wheelchairs would allow and Dave clicked away.

"C'mon, Dave! We're hungry!" Eddie complained.

"Awright, boys…just a couple more. Excellent! Let's go eat!"

The boys headed outside and immediately felt the sweltering heat and humidity.

"Boy, is it ever hot already!" Ethan groaned.

Connor chirped, "Pool's gonna feel great today!"

The covered front porch of Cabin 22 was equipped with a ramp that led the boys to the road that passed all the other similarly equipped cabins. On the other side of the road was the sidewalk that led away to the parking lots and the entrance to the camp. Cabin 22 could see all the way to the main highway.

TJ glimpsed out the entrance and asked no one in particular, "Is that where they come in?"

Mischievous Connor, sensing a chance to have some fun with his young friend, pounced and quickly offered, "Sure is. But they'll be coming out of the sky, riding on bolts of lightning, TJ!"

Dave watched as TJ's eyes gazed into the sky. He knew TJ bought Connor's little fib and responded quickly, "TJ, Connor's just tellin' stories, buddy. They'll be coming right in the entrance, right where you first looked. We'll be here waiting for them when they come."

CHAPTER

4

The gang from the north worked its way southward, staying off the main roads and instead choosing less traveled back roads. The riders enjoyed the twists and turns, the leaning through the curves, the acceleration down the straight parts and into the next turn. It was the sheer joy of the ride, being out in the world, being part of it, not just simply watching it go by. The sidecar riders enjoyed the experience too, but in a different way. Their three-wheel machines didn't take to the curves like the two-wheelers. They had to muscle their rigs around the curves, riding on their own edge of balance.

The whole group as one looked like a centipede scurrying around a woodpile as they danced down the road, each rider, his own part of the whole. So it would be when they reached their destination.

They took the road less traveled, because it was less traveled and a lot more fun. This road followed a meandering stream and it seemed the road makers wanted to mimic the stream exactly.

Big Bear, at the front of the human centipede, had been listening to the weatherband radio on his bike and had become increasingly concerned about what was happening above them. The further south they went, the worse the weather appeared to be getting, even at this early point in the day. The sun had given way to dark forbidding clouds and the wind was starting to pick up as well. He wanted to make sure the group was through "The Narrows" before any storm overtook them.

The Narrows was a treacherous section of highway that crossed the top of Eagle Mountain. Two narrow lanes, no shoulder on the side of the road, and no guiderails, made for no safe place to stop. It was a motorcyclist's paradise on a good day, filled with sharp turns, switchbacks, and steep grades. But when the road surface got wet, it became very dangerous. He had chosen this way because of the fun factor, but had realized too late that rain would surely slow them down, or possibly end the day completely.

He looked in his rearview mirror at the mass of humanity and machinery behind him. And it never ceased to amaze him how much joy he could see on the faces of the following riders. He felt proud to be leading them.

The gang pulled into a small village, nestled along the stream they had been following. Bear signaled that he was

Photo by Bjarke Johansen

stopping and pulled into the parking lot of a long-closed factory. All motors were shut off, riders jumped off their bikes and removed helmets to get some air moving around their heads. The warm, soupy air provided little respite, but after a couple hours of hard riding, a break was welcome.

Some shared water with others. The ladies made futile attempts to fix their hair. Every day with a helmet on is a bad hair day. Today, the humidity made for bad hair, even before helmets were worn. The riders congregated around Bear. He began with a smile that quickly made its way through the group.

"Ya havin' fun??" A collective head bob went through the group, following the smiles. "Good. Thought you guys would enjoy that road. That's the fun part." He paused.

"The not-so-fun part is there's a nasty storm developing to the west of us and it looks like we're gonna get wet. We gotta get up and over The Narrows before the storm hits," and he paused again, "Or we're not gonna make it today."

JD chimed in, "Oh, we got to make it today. They're counting on us to make it today! A little rain never slowed us down before, Bear!"

"I know, JD, but it's kind of a timing thing. If we're going to get there in time we gotta go up through The Narrows. And you guys know how bad that road is when it's wet, and it looks now like we'll be meeting up with the storm up on that mountain almost for sure."

"Well, what are we waiting for? Let's go!" JD was ready for any riding surface. Bear wasn't so sure about some of the others.

CHAPTER

5

The boys entered the dining hall with a flourish, thinking they would be unique with their Kings T-shirts, but it turned out other campers thought today was a good day for team spirit and most other cabin groups had their "colors" on as well.

Specially made tables that allowed places for wheelchairs to park were placed in two long rows on each side of the dining hall. Every meal began with announcements and then a selected cabin group performed some kind of skit. The campers in Cabin 4 performed *Little Deuce Coupe* by The Beach Boys, complete with choreographed wheelchair movements. At camp, nobody sees the chairs. They become invisible.

Cabin 4 was well-received and the pre-breakfast drills ended with a list of the day's activities. The camp director, Martin, stood up and the campers all whooped. "Today you guys are going to be busy. This morning, half of you are in the pool, the other half of you will be at crafts. Then you'll switch."

Connor whispered to Ethan, "Hey, I love that lift that sets me right in the water! That's cool!"

Ethan could still walk, so he used the steps into the water, but still replied, "I wish I could ride in it too!"

Martin continued, "After lunch, we have a very special event planned for you and it's looking like the Cabin 22 Sidecar Kings have a pretty good idea of what that special event is, right, boys?!"

The Kings knew better than anyone else in camp what was happening after lunch and they were more than ready.

"I don't want you guys to get your hopes too far up, though. I heard there's a bad storm coming later and our afternoon guests may have to cancel."

There was a collective groan throughout the dining hall and some vocal protesting from Shawn, "Aw, man! I wait all year for this and now you're sayin' they might not come???"

The Kings couldn't imagine a camp without sidecar rides.

"Hey, Dave," Eddie asked, "ever been to camp when the sidecars didn't come?"

"Well, Eddie, there was a camp a few years back… it rained all week. We were inside the whole time. There were no rides that week. Everything was canceled."

"That musta stunk," responded Eddie.

"It did, boy, it sure did. But nothing has been canceled yet, so make the most of the time. That's all we can do.

We can't fuss over stuff we can't do anything about, so quit worrying. You got enough to worry about already, little big man. Hear me?"

"Loud and clear, Dave."

TJ paid particular attention. His day would be ruined if there was no ride. He remained silent and hoped along with the rest of the campers their rider friends would not back down from a storm.

After grace, camp breakfast was scrambled eggs made by the gallon, cold toast and bacon, and bug juice. There was fruit, but nobody ate it. It was camp time. For the Sidecar Kings, breakfast was something to be tolerated and moved through so the next fun thing could happen. Connor tried to start a food fight, but Dave was too quick and stopped it before it started.

"Connor, I know you'd rather throw your food than eat it, but you have to remember that volunteers make our food for us and we should be grateful for what we have here."

"Dave, this bacon tastes like cardboard, is too tough to chew, and the toast is colder than ice. Nothing I can really eat but the eggs and that's not really food. It's more like plastic that has food smell added."

Dave surrendered a smile and admitted the young man had a point.

The campers were still inside the dining hall when the sun disappeared behind a bank of dark clouds.

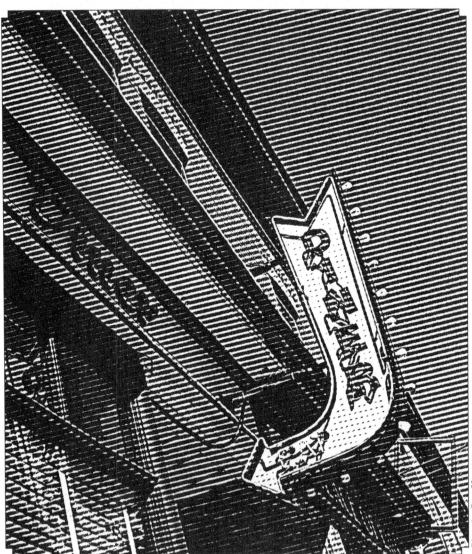

CHAPTER

6

Most of the riders from the north hadn't eaten breakfast before the ride, which made skipping an opportunity to eat an unpopular option. Bikers love to eat, whether a storm is coming or not. During the stop in the factory parking lot, Jack eyed a restaurant just up the road.

"Bear, while we're here, let's eat!"

Bear watched as universal agreement for food spread throughout the group. All pledged to keep the stop as quick as possible so they could get back on the road. He figured a few extra minutes weren't going to matter much now anyway. He knew they were going to get caught in the rain whether they ate or not.

The riders pulled into the restaurant parking lot and filled all the unfilled spots with motorcycles. Everyone dismounted and stowed their riding gear away. The ladies tried in vain to fix their 'helmet hair'. Most riders found hats to wear and ignored hair entirely.

The group went inside and was graciously welcomed by the restaurant staff. Bear had brought riders to this place for years. The staff could take on a big gang of people in short order and get them back on the road quickly.

When the riders finished their meals and left the restaurant, they discovered it had already begun raining. Small droplets appeared all over the previously mirror-finished chrome and spotless, shiny paint. All bikes had been previously washed and cleaned especially for the day.

Stretch reminded Mel as they donned their rain gear, "Want it to rain? Wash your bike!"

Jack grumbled after looking in his empty tour pack, "I forgot to bring my rain gear. I was so busy thinking about the trip, I forgot to think about what I should pack. I guess this is what I get for wanting a little breakfast."

JD was laughing. "You crazy man! Rule Number One is you never leave the house without your rain gear!"

"I know …" Jack replied sheepishly. "But I wore it the other day when I gave my dog a bath and I left it to dry in the shed. Forgot it was there."

"What, the dog or your suit?" JD joked. Several other riders overheard the comment and laughed in unison. Riding with a group allows for lots of laughing moments.

"Jack," JD offered, "you can have my suit. I have a change of clothes in the sidecar and I can change when we get there. Here you go."

"You're all right," Jack replied gratefully. He then took JD's rain suit and quickly got into it.

Bear was the last one to leave the restaurant. As was the custom, he picked up the tab for the group for the meal. The man was as generous as they came. He walked over to Jack and JD and the group quickly closed in around them.

"Folks," he began, "we have an important choice to make here. Either we go back home and make ourselves no-shows, but significantly reduce the risk factor, or we keep going and hope the worst of this weather gets by us before we get up and over Eagle Mountain. Either way, we're gonna get wet."

The riders looked around at one another and then at Bear. Froggy reported, "Don't know about you guys, but I'm for going ahead. JD, you stand to get the wettest, what do you think?"

"I'm afraid I'm not a good, wise person to ask," JD said. "I ride every day. I've ridden in snow, sleet, freezing rain, and rain so heavy that cows were floating across the highway." The group laughed.

"I've also ridden The Narrows when it was wet. You're gonna really need to keep your heads up there. It is no place for faint-hearted souls. If we go ahead, we need to take it real easy and be careful. And, Froggy, it's only water. I can get dry later."

"Ok, then. We keep going," Bear added. "But if you feel unsure, the time to say so is now, not up on those switchbacks. If you want to go back, nobody will blame you. Anybody goin' back?"

Again the group looked at one another and responded with silence.

"JD, since you seem to have the most alternative surface experience, you lead us up through. Take it easy, and keep us tight. I'm gonna stay back and ride near some of the newer guys and help 'em out when it hits the fan up there."

"I'll keep us tight for sure. I promise, Bear." JD immediately realized he had been bestowed a huge responsibility. He vowed not to let his friends down.

The riders mounted, the rain began to pick up in intensity, the wind pushed the leaves to show their backs, and lightning, hidden so far from clear view, flashed inside the advancing storm clouds.

While the group readied itself, Bear's daughter, Cherie, had run inside the restaurant and retrieved a garbage bag for JD to slip into. He cut a hole for his head and arms and slipped it over his head. He and Bear switched places and the gang of wet Harleys rumbled to life.

Eagle Mountain was just a few miles in the distance. Dark, angry clouds already hid the summit.

JD was resigned. "We're getting through that," he muttered to himself. "Come hell or high water, we're getting through that. And I bet we'll see both up there."

JD pulled out his cell phone to text an alert to his buddy, Dave, at the camp that the riders might be delayed. He thought his text went through, but he didn't have time to check. With that, a bolt of lightning streaked from the sky in front of them, followed by an ear-splitting crack of thunder, as if daring the riders to pass through its fury. JD looked over his shoulder, saw he was being followed, lowered his face shield and led his friends into the storm.

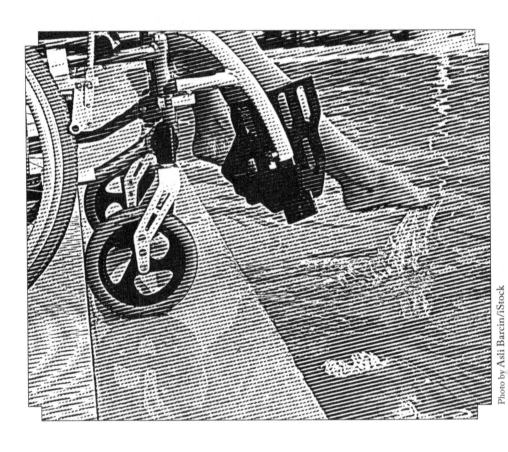

CHAPTER

7

As the Kings left the dining hall, they made a beeline to the pool. They all dressed in their bathing suits when they woke, so they were ready. Since four of the five campers from Cabin 22 were wheelchair-bound, the lift was needed to get them in the water. The counselors were trained how to use the lift and gently lowered each camper into the water, into the waiting arms of another counselor. The one place an MDA camper feels more at home than in a wheelchair is in the water.

Connor's yellow floatation collar was bobbing colorfully in the warm water. He enjoyed being dunked. Although Ethan was able to help himself into the water, he still wore a preserver as well. He and his counselor splashed each other. Eddie, Shawn, and TJ created a preserver flotilla and imagined they were the US Naval Special Forces, taking on all enemies.

Other cabins soon joined the fun. The pool was the

place to be.

Martin, the camp director, was sitting in his office when he heard the rain beginning to fall on the tin roof above him. A long-time area director for the MDA, Martin had the perfect temperament for the demanding camp director's position. He adored the kids and worked very hard alongside the rest of the staff to make sure every kid's camping experience could be the best it could be. He'd been checking the weather throughout the morning and realized that it wouldn't be long before the storm would worsen. Lightning and lots of wheelchair-bound kids in the pool didn't make safe sense.

He checked the weather radar on the TV one last time before heading out to the pool. A band of green, with imbedded bands of orange and red crossed the little TV screen in his office. The blob was headed straight for the camp. The National Weather Service had issued emergency measures for a severe thunderstorm approaching the area. The emergency broadcast system had been activated, but he was already out the door.

Dave saw him first, waving his arms and yelling. But the kids were having so much fun in the water, Martin was impossible to hear. Finally he burst through the pool fence gate and blew a whistle.

The campers all stopped at once.

"Everyone out of the pool! There's a storm coming. When you get out, please head over to the recreation hall. Counselors, if you can lift your campers, please do so. We'll use the lift only for the kids that really need it." Martin was calm, but authoritative.

The counselors did as they were told. Connor was the heaviest of the boys in Cabin 22 and was the only one who really needed the lift. Dave and two other counselors worked together to get Connor and the rest of the kids out of the water and back into their chairs.

The rain began to pick up as well as the wind. The kids by now were aware that what was happening was serious and they dutifully did as they were told.

Ethan walked beside TJ as they made their way to the rec hall. "Hey, TJ, this is pretty cool! Look how black the sky is getting!"

As TJ looked up over the rec hall he could hear distant rolling thunder. "Is that them? Is that them? Are they here?"

Shawn rolled by and broke the news, "TJ, the riders are gonna cancel. There's no way they can make it through a storm like this."

"No way. I don't believe it," TJ shot back.

"Believe it, man. They're not comin'."

"You guys said last night, they come every year! They have to come. I can't miss my first ride!"

Dave ran up to the boys and helped to move them along a little faster. "Come on, boys, no messin' around now. Let's get inside."

TJ was beside himself. "Dave, Shawn said the riders canceled. Please tell me it's not true! I swear I thought I just heard them! I know I just heard the bikes!"

"That was real thunder, TJ, not Harley thunder," Dave replied.

"Tell you what. One of my buddies was supposed to ride in with that gang today. I'll see if I can get through to him. My guess is they got a mess on their hands too, but I'll try. Don't worry, little bro, it's all good."

The campers all safely reached the rec hall, as the leading edge of the storm closed in on the camp. When Dave got inside, he checked his cell and realized he'd already received a message- 'Bad storm on Eagle Mtn- att..' He was hoping his buddy JD was just having trouble with his cell phone. But he knew better.

CHAPTER

8

Eagle Mountain, according to local folklore, had a mystical history. The Native Americans who once lived in the area claimed the mountain to be sacred. This was the place where the eagle, the messenger of the creator, came from the heavens in a great storm cloud and landed here. The flash of lightning and the roar of thunder was its call. The majestic creature landed in the tall trees at the summit. He then lifted again and descended softly to the ground. As he approached the earth, according to the legend, he reached out his talon and when he stepped on the ground became a man. (D'Arcy Rheault from http://www.angelfire.com/ca/Indian/EagleStories.html.)

The mountain also happened to be in the path of an eagle and hawk migration flyway. When the weather was clear, bird watchers from all over came to catch glimpses of brown tails, coopers, and even bald eagles.

JD noticed the traffic coming off the mountain. He

figured the bird watchers had been chased by the storm.

"Smart ones," he thought to himself. "They are fleeing in four wheels and we're riding straight into the teeth of this monster on motorcycles."

Already soaked to the skin, the garbage bag he attempted to use for rain gear simply channeled the water onto his body. He felt as if he was riding inside a dishwasher. The thought made him smile. "No shower needed today!" he said to himself.

As he approached the first of many steep switchbacks, he took quick stock of the situation. On a sidecar, JD had the added safety of a third wheel, but had less room to move.

Photo by Dimitri Castrique Ploegsteert

The two-wheelers had more room to move, but needed it to maintain balance through the ever-increasing puddles. He then looked in his rear view mirrors and saw nothing but water droplets and a faint suggestion of the headlights of the bikes behind. He lifted his face shield and turned to glance behind him and discovered the group was right behind him.

Like a pair of fighter jets in combat, Jack stayed right on JD's right rear quarter. He looked almost comfortable in borrowed rain gear. Was that a smile on Jack's face?

"Atta boy, Jack," JD said to himself. "Hang close, hold on tight, and keep smilin' and we'll get through this. That rain gear I loaned you sure looks comfy right now!"

The wind had begun to sway the tops of the heavy trees. Small twigs had begun to appear on the roadway as the trees danced in the storm. The brunt of the wind, thankfully, hadn't reached the road yet. The riding was slow, but still progressing.

Cracks of thunder and streaks of lightning now were happening every few seconds and the rain came harder. The weather sounds had overtaken the bike sounds as the storm increased in intensity.

Moving water replaced the puddles in spots and the riders had to slow down to work their way through the water making its way unabated down the mountain road.

As the determined riders ascended the mountain, the

storm's full fury was unleashed. Falling twigs became larger branches, as the trees whipped wildly from side to side. Leaves and debris swirled around the riders and the wind pushed the big machines relentlessly.

Suddenly, without warning, a falling branch the size of a man's index finger glanced off JD's windshield and momentarily frightened him.

"This is madness," JD thought to himself. The kids were waiting for them, but there wouldn't be much riding happening if all the bikes were wrecked. The water and the wind were coming straight on and visibility was just a few feet.

He looked for a clearing to stop and wait out the rest of the storm. He knew the riders behind him would continue as long as he did, but would have followed him to a safe place to stop, without argument now. As they rounded the next bend, nature had decided for them. A massive tree had fallen across the road and they had to stop.

The riders pulled up to the fallen tree and looked on with amazement. The massive pin oak was 60 feet tall and easily 25 feet wide. Froggy hopped off his bike and was curiously drawn to the fallen tree. He stepped inside the canopy and promptly disappeared. He appeared shortly afterward and as if on his own personal expedition, reported with a smile that it was reasonably dry within the leaves. The rain continued to fall and the wind gusted through The Narrows. The riders now separated from their bikes and wanted only to get out of the rain. Each rider slowly entered the opening Froggy had entered shortly before.

Inside the big tree's canopy, it was indeed drier than standing out in the pouring rain. The large oak branches that weren't smashed in the fall to the road made reasonable seats for the drenched bikers to sit on. The group began to realize the tree had offered something to them totally unexpected. All quietly prayed a word of thanks the tree hadn't fallen a few seconds later. Anyone under the tree when it fell would have never survived.

The gang listened to the wind whip around them and the rain spray the outer leaves, but remarkably, the unexpected shelter was reasonably weather-tight. It gave them all time to take in what was happening.

After a few moments, Jack broke the silence, "So what's the plan now? If we go back to the main highway, we won't get to the camp until the evening."

Bear was uncharacteristically resigned but still smiling that Big Bear smile, "This storm is a doozie. Good bet there's damage all over. We're lucky nobody got hurt yet. Once things calm down, we'll get ourselves cleaned up and head back home. We tried, folks. We tried."

CHAPTER

9

The campers all crowded into the rec center just before the brunt of the storm hit. With a limited number of windows and strong concrete construction, the building served the camp well in many capacities. Today, a gang of children, most all of whom were in some kind of wheelchair, called it refuge. As the storm whipped its fury onto the camp grounds, the counselors were concerned the kids would be scared.

Dave's cool, easy attitude was a huge help, though. It also didn't hurt that he was a firefighter. Firefighters and the MDA have a special bond to begin with. Firefighters across the country annually raise enormous amounts of money for Jerry's Kids, for the MDA. They have sent countless kids to camp and have provided millions of dollars to the MDA research effort over the years.

The kids gathered in their groups and talked among themselves. The counselors had worked hard not to panic the kids. Their hard work paid off. But just as the inside of the building began to settle, the wind drove the branch of a large sycamore tree into one of the center's few windows. The branch couldn't come through because the windows had been covered with steel screens so errant basketballs could not damage from the inside.

The glass fell harmlessly outside the building, but the wind howled through the steel screen. Again, when Dave thought there would be panic, the kids simply mimicked the sound in whatever way they could.

Some whistled, some yelled, some used wheelchair horns to overpower the windy noise.

"Amazing," he thought. "These kids are amazing."

CHAPTER

10

The riders, all still in their rain gear and helmets, joking joyfully among themselves, hadn't realized they weren't alone. In the deepest reaches of the now-fallen tree, the branches and leaves gradually fell together as the rain and the wind pressed upon them. Within the mass of green foliage was another surprise.

A wild screech rolled through the leaves into the temporary sanctuary. At the far top side of the tree the group made out the silhouette of a large bald eagle. The bird screeched again and disappeared.

"Guess she's lookin' for some dry too, huh, JD?" Froggy pondered.

"Don't know, Froggy. She coulda' been here the whole time. Hope she doesn't have a nest in this tree."

Before JD could finish the words, explorer Froggy had disappeared into the foliage. He came back a short time later and reported that there was a nest, or what was left of one, towards the end of the main trunk.

Even though an eagle's nest is notoriously strong, it would be tough for any nest to stay together as the tree it was built in was blown to the ground.

JD asked, "Didja see any other birds in there?"

"Yea. Mama was either crying 'cuz her house got smashed or rejoicin' 'cuz she didn't lose 'er young 'uns." He continued, "We're sharing a tree with three eagles! "

Above the wind and rain another sound slowly worked its way into the huddled gang.

"Sounds like a car or truck motor," Jack reported.

"Diesel truck," Bear corrected. He could name the sound of virtually any vehicle on the road.

"It sounds like he's above us. He must've come from the other side of The Narrows. And that means that if there's a way to get around this tree, we might be able to keep going!"

In all the commotion the eagles had caused, the group hadn't realized the rain had begun to let up. The group of soggy riders slowly worked their way toward the noisy diesel truck. Turns out, it was a diesel pickup, like Bear had declared.

The driver couldn't believe his eyes as all the riders stepped out of the foliage of the fallen tree on his side. The drenched riders looked like a band of colorful astronauts.

He rolled down his window and looked into Bear's

smiling cheerful face. "You guys aren't hiking around in that gear, are ya? Didja lose your mother ship in the storm?"

Bear laughed the only way Bear can and responded, "Ha! Naw, wise guy! We got about 20 motorcycles on the opposite side of this tree. We were headed to the MDA camp in the next valley when the storm hit and blew this tree onto the road in front of us."

"Man, oh, man, you guys are either really brave, or really crazy to be riding in weather like this," the pickup driver said. "I've never seen a storm hit so quick and so hard like that. The road is clear from here up, but barely. I was at the summit when the storm let loose. I put my winch cable around one of those big oaks up there and just held on tight. I figured if the tree let go, I would go with it. Good thing I didn't attach myself to this one. I'd be under it now! "

Bear nodded and responded, "Any chance that winch you got up front can help us make a path?"

"Better than that," the driver cheerfully beamed. "I got a saw. I can cut you a path. With a little help we can cut you a slot in no time!"

"We'll need a pretty big slot," Bear added. "We got a couple sidecar rigs that need to squeeze through, too."

"Sidecars… you guys headed to the camp to give rides?" The pickup truck driver asked.

Bear smiled.

"Ah. My kid was a camper a few years ago. You guys from Big's Harley up in Pleasantville, by any chance?"

Bear replied, "Yup! That's us!"

The driver continued, "One of your guys gave him a ride. Actually think it was a woman on the motorcycle. My son never forgot that ride."

"That was probably one of my daughters who gave your son his ride. They are both here somewhere," Bear beamed. He was very proud of his offspring.

"What's your name, driver?" Bear inquired.

"I'm Jon."

"Well, pleasure there, Jon. If you can help us get through this hunk of wood, I'd be obliged to ya. By the way, what are you doin' up this way, anyway?"

"Bird watching," Jon said. "Coulda' swore I heard a 'baldy' not too long ago."

"Have I got a bird story for you..." Bear chuckled. And as the pickup truck driver got his saw ready, Bear related the amazing story of the eagles.

Jon began clearing the smaller outer branches first. He was careful to avoid the area where Bear thought the eagles were perched. What he had not known was that the eagles had made a hasty exit after Froggy had found them.

In a few minutes, a single path was cleared. With the help of other riders, the road was soon clear enough for them all to pass.

After the bikes were through the tree, Bear stopped and thanked Jon the only way he knew how.

"Hey, Jon, next time you're up around Pleasantville with your son, bring him by the store. We'll be glad to take him and you for a ride."

"You can count on me to take you up on that offer, Bear!" Jon responded excitedly.

The group exchanged grateful "thank yous" and handshakes, and continued on their way.

Photo by Thomas C.

CHAPTER
11

The campers were making so much noise inside the rec center, no one realized the storm had blown itself out and the first rays of sun appeared through the battered windows. Dave and a couple other counselors cautiously opened the front doors to see what kind of damage the storm had caused.

From their vantage point they could see lots of downed limbs, and leaves strewn about. Decorations from the cabin porches were littered everywhere. The pool had become a depository for the lounge chairs that had originally been placed around the pool. The wind neatly cleaned the area, blowing everything in its path into the pool.

Dave mused, "Could've been a lot worse, I suppose. Nothing we can't fix, from what I can see."

Martin had been standing with the counselors and concurred. "Yea. We are lucky... oh, wait a minute. Something doesn't look right over at the picnic pavilion."

All eyes found the pavilion and tried to reorganize the

scene before the storm.

"Oh, boy," Dave lamented. "The big old maple that was next to the pavilion is now on top of the pavilion. Looks like the roof down there is badly damaged."

"We still are lucky," Martin replied cheerfully. "We can continue camp. We can work without the pavilion. The camp crew can get the place back in shape in no time. Our biggest challenge now is the gap we have in the schedule this afternoon."

Dave cautioned, "The riders surely must have bailed. I have a kid in my cabin that was really looking forward to his first sidecar ride."

"Not so fast, Dave," Martin said. "Never underestimate a Harley rider on a mission. I've been trying to raise them since the middle of the storm but haven't had any luck."

"I got a cryptic message from JD," Dave replied. "They must've weathered the storm on Eagle Mountain. They were trying to make time through The Narrows when the storm hit up there. I only got part of his text message, though. Cell service isn't very good up there even on a good day."

Martin had also received a text message from Bear, saying the same thing. "They would never leave us hanging without any kind of contact."

"...unless something happened to them all," Dave finished.

Martin grimaced at that thought and headed down to check out the pavilion damage. Dave and the rest of the counselors went back inside to release the kids into the storm-battered camp. They would never forget this day.

When Dave returned inside, the campers were already waiting at the door. When he gave the "all clear", they all scampered out any way they could. It reminded him of toll booth traffic at rush hour... 8 lanes into 2, as all the wheelchairs jockeyed for position to get through the doorway.

Looking past the rush, he saw one camper who hadn't moved towards the door. TJ was facing the corner as if he was being punished. Dave made his way through the throng at the doorway and walked across the now-empty rec center floor.

"Hey, TEE! Let's get out of here. We'll head back to the cabin and whip up some of those marshmallow smoothies you told us about last night!" Dave could see TJ was trying miserably to hold back tears.

"I don't feel like going back to the cabin, Dave. There's nuthin' to do there 'cept talk about stuff that'll never happen. All the guys got me excited for a ride in a sidecar and now that's not gonna happen. You can't be a Sidecar King unless you rode in a sidecar."

"Ah! So that's the reason for the long face! Ya know, TJ, there's no crying allowed at camp! And as for the sidecar rides, I don't know for sure, buddy, but I suspect that'll all take care of itself," Dave offered.

"Dave, how do you know so much about everything?" TJ angrily jabbed back.

Dave hesitated for a moment and looked away. TJ looked up and noticed Dave was choking back his own tears. "Dave, I'm sorry, I didn't mean to…"

"Nah, it's ok, buddy. It's just that I haven't heard those words in years. My kid brother used to say that to me all the time. In fact, you remind me a lot of him."

"Was he in a wheelchair, too, Dave, like me?"

"Yup. He had SMA too."

"Where is he now, Dave? How come he isn't at camp with you?"

"TJ, my brother is in Heaven now. He passed away about 10 years ago. He got real sick one winter, and he never got better."

After a long silence, TJ replied, "A couple campers told me the other day we were really lucky to have you as a counselor, that you were special, somehow. They said anybody could tell you were cool, just by looking at your eyes. So that's the story behind your eyes…isn't it?"

Dave smiled gently, "Yea, that could be it."

"What do ya think's going to happen to me, to Connor, to the rest of the guys?" TJ asked without fear and quite matter-of-factly.

Wiping away the last tear, Dave replied, "Don't know, buddy. I don't know. But I do know you can sit there and think about how crappy everything is and let it take you down, or you can get ready for the next something special. It's your choice. It's up to you, little man."

After some pondering, TJ replied, "Dave, there's no crying allowed in camp."

Dave laughed quietly again and said finally, "Ya got me good that time! Keep this between you and me, TJ. Got it?"

"Got it, Dave. Oh, one other thing."

"What's that, TJ?"

"Thanks, Dave. Thanks for everything."

"No, buddy. Thank you."

Dave nodded toward the rec center doors and said, "You should see the camp. Looks like a small tornado went through out there. We're lucky nobody got hurt. Let's head back to the cabin. I sure hope we didn't leave any windows open!"

TJ finally cracked a smile and joined Dave and the two headed back to the cabin together.

CHAPTER

12

Big Bear had resumed leading the riders and was trying to make up for some lost time. Miraculously, no man, woman, or machine had sustained any serious damage. Bear thanked his lucky stars. Bear was not the kind of man who would ever put someone in harm's way on purpose. He was very relieved none of his friends got hurt.

As they continued into the valley, he spotted a local police car sitting along the side of the road. He raised his hand and gave the "all- stop" signal and the riders all pulled up behind him.

At first, the cop was a bit unsure about what was unfolding behind him. Bear dismounted from his bike and walked up to the open window. He flashed a huge smile. "Hey, there, officer! We're headed to the MDA camp down the road. These sidecar rigs behind me should have campers in 'em by now. We got a little sidetracked up on Eagle Mountain because of the storm." Bear paused to check for the officer's reaction. "Any chance you can help us make some noise so those kids down there know we're coming?"

The cop slowly broke into a knowing smile. "I know you- you're Big Bear, aren't you?"

"Well, yea, sometimes. You can call me anything you want, though. Just don't call me late for dinner!" Bear poked his own belly and waited for a moment and then added, "Real fond of that time of day!" The riders behind him all laughed out loud at the obvious comment.

The officer looked at Bear's size and again at his big smile and instantly became a fan. "Bear, I'll do even better than that. I'll escort you there myself."

The cop switched on his lights, pulled out onto the road and waited for all the riders to remount their iron horses and position themselves behind him. When everyone was ready, he activated the sirens and the parade began.

CHAPTER

13

TJ was sitting on the Cabin 22 porch with Connor and the two were laughing about the furniture in the pool, when TJ first heard the sound.

"Ya hear that, Connor?"

"Hear what, the sirens?"

"No! The rumble... that low rumbling sound..."

"Sheesh, TJ, all I hear is sirens....wait. I DO hear a rumble...sounds like rolling thunder! Ya know what that is, TJ?"

"Harley motorcycles," he said in a whisper, then raising his voice in disbelief, "They MADE it, Connor!!! The Harleys are comin' after all!"

They saw the flashing lights on top of the police car first. Their ears had already picked up the siren and they could almost feel the rumble of the bikes before they actually heard them. As the police car turned into the camp entrance, TJ could see motorcycle headlights following closely behind.

His earlier dismay turned to unbridled joy. "They're here, Connor. Oh, man, they made it through the storm! How cool is that?"

Connor looked on and smiled. "Hey, kid, it's kinda' like I said after all, huh? They're not riding in from the sky on a bolt of lightning, but this is pretty close!"

Bear was the first bike behind the police escort, followed by the seven sidecars in single file, and then the remaining riders.

The bikers took a parade lap around the camp access road, waving, beeping their horns and revving their motors as they made their way past their camp friends. TJ and Connor were on the porch of Cabin 22 when the riders slowly went by. The counselors and the boys had just rehung their Cabin 22- Sidecar Kings banner.

Connor and TJ were soon joined by Eddie, Shawn, Ethan, and Dave. They all waved and gave the thumbs up to the riders. Their sign seemed to get a lot of extra attention.

TJ saw one sidecar that stood out from the others. His friends told him to look for a black sidecar that looked like part of a fighter jet. They told him that sidecar was attached to a Harley-Davidson Road King, the only Road King motorcycle in the bunch.

TJ knew that he was now looking at that special machine. The boys left the porch and headed to the loading zone where all the riders were parking. TJ went straight for the jet black ride. "My friends at home will never believe this!" he said to no one in particular. He was about to become a member of a very exclusive club.

Dave remained on the porch and pulled out his camera as he watched TJ wheel his way to the waiting rigs. He clicked off a couple of pictures.

He thought to himself, "I'm gonna send that one to Webster's Dictionary and tell them to use that photo to portray the word 'joy'." He ran to join the rest of his cabin. The real fun was just beginning.

Photo by Jon Burcaw

CHAPTER

14

The seven sidecar rigs parked in a row made an impressive sight, even after such an eventful, wet ride. The riders had all dismounted and prepared their sidecars for passengers. Six of the rigs had simple vinyl covers over the compartment of the passenger seat. The seventh rig, the "King", had a cover complete with side and rear windows. Riders could actually ride under the cover while the motorcycle was in operation. But no one ever did. It was too much fun to ride with the cover off.

Once TJ's sidecar cover was removed, he looked into the torpedo-shaped body and the jet fighter-style, swooped back windshield that created the cockpit where he would sit. He caught his own reflection in the jet black paint of the body. It reminded him of the time he was wheeling past a fun house mirror. His reflection looked almost cartoonlike.

The seat was deep inside the passenger compartment. The opening was big enough for two people to sit comfortably.

TJ would need the extra room. Since he couldn't hold himself up, he needed to sit on a grownup's lap. As he continued to marvel at the amazing machine before him, he didn't realize he was now surrounded by other riders.

JD released two chrome clips on each side of the cockpit and the upper half of the nose of the sidecar body began to slowly rotate upward. TJ could hear the quiet hiss of two gas shocks controlling the opening.

JD looked at TJ's face and could see the clear fascination with the strange machine. TJ's eyes widened, "Whoa.... Cool!"

There in front of him was the now-accessible seat and a black-carpeted floor. All the obstacles of his ride were fading away.

"What's your name, son?" JD asked, smiling. TJ responded with a whisper. "What was that???" JD asked again.

"Uh, sorry!!! My name's TJ and I love this motorcycle! It's the coolest machine I ever saw!"

"Yea, this is a pretty cool machine, TJ. My name's JD. Wanna take a ride?"

"Oh, boy! Could I?"

"Wanna bring a buddy with you? There's enough room in there for you and your best camp buddy. Who's your buddy this week, TJ?"

"Uh, my buddy...Dave is my counselor buddy this week. He'll ride with me for sure!"

Dave had worked his way around the other riders and was now at TJ's side. "You been waiting a long while for this moment, haven't you, buddy?" Dave said.

"Dave, I can't believe it's finally happening."

Dave knew the drill. Campers who couldn't ride alone needed a buddy to ride with them to be safe. He climbed into the sidecar seat first so TJ could be placed on his lap. In the meantime, two other riders carefully lifted TJ out of his wheelchair and into Dave's arms.

Kids who live in wheelchairs all of their lives become very accustomed to the safety their chair provides. And even when the caregiver is a well-known family member, transfer from the chair to any other place can be frightening. TJ overcame his fear of being lifted by total strangers and being placed in Dave's lap. He carefully instructed the attentive riders exactly how they should hold him.

Once in place, TJ's smile returned once again. The riders brought with them a number of helmets, as all campers by rule needed to wear one. Jack found a nice orange helmet and gently placed it on TJ's head.

"Ok, TJ! You're all fastened in!" Jack announced. Dave pulled the seat belt over the both of them and clicked the two ends together. The two riders, who loaded TJ into the sidecar then closed the uplifted nose and latched it into place.

TJ's heart was pounding as the windshield closed over him. He was safely inside the sidecar now.

JD turned the ignition switch on the bike to the "on" position and pressed the starter. The big motorcycle roared to life. The sound the bike made and the vibration of the engine created the feeling of movement even before the machine began rolling.

He looked down to TJ and said, "Only one rule on this motorcycle today and that's to have some fun. Ya ready to roll?"

"You bet, JD! Let's go!"

CHAPTER

15

Just before TJ began moving, he looked over to his right and saw the rest of Cabin 22. Connor, Eddie, Shawn, and Ethan all in a bunch, had their thumbs high in the air, saluting the newest member of the Sidecar Kings as he rolled out for his inaugural ride.

JD saw the salute and blew the horn on the big Harley in happy response and finally got under way.

"How ya doin', TJ?" Dave asked in his ear.

"Great, Dave! This is awesome!"

JD departed from the loading lane, took a left at the camp caretaker's house and made his way down towards the damaged picnic pavilion. The camp crew had cleared all the camp paths of any limbs or objects that had been blown around by the storm, but JD took his time anyway.

Along the path stood a large group of similarly dressed volunteers who had come to spend time with the kids. They stood along the path and clapped their hands and whistled as the first passenger of the day went by. They cheered for the kids and for the riders alike.

JD continued past the pavilion and they briefly viewed the tree that had dropped on the pavilion roof. He was quickly reminded of the fallen tree he and his friends had used for shelter on their journey over Eagle Mountain. "Wow!" he said above the noise of the bike. "Looks like you guys got the same storm we did on our way here!"

TJ looked past JD and saw the splintered pavilion roof and the fallen tree. He was amazed the structure was still standing. "Good thing we weren't under there, huh, Dave? We woulda' been squashed like bugs!"

"For sure, buddy, for sure!"

As the sidecar rig continued on the path around the dining hall, JD had noticed the rec center double doors had been left open. He aimed his machine toward the doorway.

For a moment TJ was incredulous. He yelled up to JD, "You're not goin' inside there, are ya? We're not gonna fit through!"

"Sure, we will, buddy! Hold on tight!" And they motored inside.

The trio motored in circles around the inside of the rec center. As centrifugal force slowly pushed on the riders, Dave held on to TJ a little tighter. "Whoa, buddy! This is like riding in a roller coaster!"

TJ responded, "Wahoo! Faster, faster! Hey, Dave! We're riding inside!"

JD obliged simply by pulling in the clutch and revving the motor, making it seem the machine was moving faster when actually they were slowing down. After a couple more tight turns inside the rec center and some ear-splitting throttle blasts, JD headed for the exit, and sunlight.

"That was awesome!!! Let's do it again!" TJ was a constant smile. The sidecar made a right turn after leaving the rec center and continued on.

The path now had become crowded with volunteers who had come after the storm and campers who were making their way to the sidecar loading zone. JD had to be careful how he navigated the bike. The trio came upon the camp cabins. Sitting on Cabin 22's porch was bike rider Stretch and his wife, Mel, with a camera and an instant printer. JD pulled the rig up to the cabin porch and stopped so TJ could have his picture taken.

Just like the hundreds of riders before him, TJ beamed a real, genuine, heartfelt smile for the camera that was born from the soul of an amazing machine.

CHAPTER

16

JD, Dave, and TJ followed the camp path until it ended in the middle of a grassy area near the camp indoor pool. Again, TJ gasped as JD continued rolling past the end of the path and motored into the grass. JD pointed the machine towards an earthen bridge over a swale. The terrain became rougher as JD crossed the bridge and followed the suggestion of an old path through a meadow. He slowed the rig down to keep his passengers from getting too jostled about and to give them more time to take in the beautiful surroundings.

TJ was now in an area of camp he had not been with his wheelchair and he watched as the local birds scattered and dove around the sidecar as it passed. The machine rumbled effortlessly through the grass. Dave held onto TJ and could feel the young boy's heart beating through his tiny ribcage.

"Ya all right, buddy?" Dave asked his favorite camper of all time.

"Yea, I sure am. This is the best ever!"

JD looked down at the two smiling passengers as the sidecar King performed its magic. He marveled at how the magic worked on each of its many passengers. And he couldn't help but smile himself.

The meadow grew to the edge of a forest. The camp owners had paved a path into the woods so the kids could gain access with their wheelchairs. TJ recognized the path opening into the canopy of trees and said above the rumble of the engine, "I know where we are now. We came back here for a campfire the other night. It's spooky here in the nighttime."

The path meandered in an imperfect circle around the inside of the forest. JD expertly navigated the path barely wide enough for the bike and the sidecar. He had ridden many times on this path during previous camp visits. He could see the darkened ground of the fire pit within the circle. He also noticed some fallen trees he hadn't seen on his last visit. He presumed the morning storm was the culprit.

The sidecar followed the path until suddenly JD yanked the handlebars hard to the right and the machine lurched into an overgrown opening. TJ was about to yell in protest until he saw JD had turned into a seldom-used trail that emptied the three out onto another meadow.

The sidecar was headed toward a short but steep grassy mound. JD knew from previous experience the mound looked steeper and taller than it actually was and he just needed to make sure he kept his speed up to crest the top.

"Here comes the rollercoaster ride again, TJ- hold on, buddy!" TJ whooped as his stomach jumped along with the sidecar ascending the small, grassy hill quickly. "That was fun! Let's do that again!" TJ laughed out loud.

After ascending the hill, the terrain flattened out, and the camp parking lot came into view. JD aimed the sidecar through the cars parked in the lot and asked TJ if he was finished or if he wanted to go some more.

"More! Go around again! Can we, JD?"

JD simply smiled and aimed the rig back out into the flat meadow. JD could see other sidecars riding through the camp now. Each time they passed another rig, everyone waved to each other. The three made their way back into the paved circle in the woods and then worked their way back to where they started. They passed the volunteers again, and went into the rec center again. This time, two other sidecars were already inside and JD, Dave, and TJ joined the others in a game of "Follow the Leader." Three sidecars followed each other in a perfect circle inside the rec center. The sound of not one, but three Harleys spinning inside a building was deafening, but the campers didn't seem to mind. Then, as if on cue, the three bikes took turns heading out the door.

JD pointed the sidecar back to the loading zone,

knowing many more campers were waiting for their chance to ride. As they headed back, he told TJ what was going on.

"TJ, we're going back to give someone else a chance to ride. If ya want, and there's time at the end, you can go again. Ok, buddy?"

As they slowed to a stop, JD turned off the engine. Two other waiting riders unlatched the hinged top of the sidecar and lifted it away from TJ and Dave.

Dave released the seat belt and helped guide TJ's little body, as the riders removed the younger passenger from the sidecar and placed him carefully back in his wheelchair.

"Thank you very, very much for taking me for a ride today, JD. That was awesome."

"It sure was, JD, thank you a lot!" Dave added.

"You guys are most welcome," JD replied. "Believe me, I had as much fun as you did."

Before JD could say anything more, another camper was getting ready to take a turn in the sidecar King. And the magic was set to begin again.

TJ waited patiently for almost two hours for his second ride until all the other campers got their turn. After his first amazing ride, TJ would have waited twice as long to get another. He and Dave were JD's last ride for the day.

After all campers had their fill, the riders from the north said their goodbyes and headed back with another hefty helping of camp memories.

Bear sublimely understated the obvious just before they left, "We're taking the long way home, gang. We'll get home when we get home. One interesting Eagle Mountain crossing is enough for one day!" The riders joined him in a great laugh, got their bikes under way and left the camp in a massive display of sound and color, disappearing finally down the road they came in on.

That night, the boys of Cabin 22 stayed up late, ate snacks, and talked about the memory-filled day. This time, another voice chimed in. TJ recounted his amazing rides with a smile that simply could not be outdone by his friends. TJ was now a full-fledged member of the Sidecar Kings, the coolest name for the coolest cabin in camp, maybe the coolest cabin ever. Dave simply listened as the magic of the ride continued to work long, long into the night.

AFTERWORD

The Muscular Dystrophy Association is a voluntary national health agency — a dedicated partnership between scientists and concerned citizens aimed at conquering neuromuscular diseases that affect more than a million Americans. The MDA provides its members with a variety of programs that aim to educate, advocate, heal, and just have fun. These programs include a network of topnotch clinics, support groups, and financial aid for medical devices. Worldwide research efforts to find a cure are funded continuously. They also provide a free week of camp to all MDA kids aged 6-18. Almost all funds raised by the MDA are from private contributors.

My son, Shane, is one of those million Americans. Born with Spinal Muscular Atrophy, one of the 43 neuromuscular diseases beneath the Muscular Dystrophy umbrella, Shane never walked. He learned to drive a powered wheelchair when he was three years old. At this writing, he is a hard-working freshman in college, studying journalism and writing. Truly, his story is awe-inspiring.

Shane attended MDA camp on a few occasions.

Although he was not an avid camper, his involvement helped foster an amazing relationship with our family and the family at Schaeffer's Harley-Davidson in Orwigsburg, PA. The Schaeffers have become annual contributors to the MDA cause, raising almost $2.5 million since 1988.

One of the camp highlights for many MDA kids at the local camps is the arrival of the sidecar gang from Schaeffer's. This group spends an afternoon during the week of camp, giving rides to all campers. Through the generosity of this amazing family, I have been blessed with a one-of-a-kind daily ride…a 2004 Harley-Davidson Road King with a sidecar built perfectly for MDA campers, and for commuting back and forth to work. With this awesome machine, I have taken part in many camp rides in the last few years. Shane's had his share of rides in it too. I can safely say that there would be a heated, lively debate if we ever needed to decide who benefited more from the rides… the campers or the riders.

Unfortunately, the future of the iconic Harley-Davidson factory-made sidecar appears to be grim. Retail demand for the unique option has been declining for several years. As a result, the Motor Company made the decision in the summer of 2010 to cease production, ending a 96-year run. In time, these already-rare rigs will become collector's items and will eventually disappear completely. The sidecar will, however, remain a proud part of the Company's heritage. But as long as it runs and is in my hands, the sidecar King will continue to make MDA camp visits.

I have met some unforgettable camp kids and have been involved in some equally unforgettable camp rides, in all kinds of weather. Some have joked that I have a penchant for bringing the rain with me. Since I began riding along, the weather has grown wetter, I've been told. But it would take a monsoon to keep the riders from Schaeffer's from their annual pilgrimage. Even then, most riders would rather get wet than let the kids down.

While there is some yarn spun in the making of this unlikely patchwork quilt, there is more real, than not. To prove my point, I will gladly take you on the next camp ride myself and show you where real smiles come from. Just bring your rain gear. You will surely need it. JB

Real campers, real riders: *page 76: Cody Duckinfield in the sidecar, Donald Snyder on the bike; page 83: Alexander Pearse in the sidecar, author Jon Burcaw on the bike; page 68: riders Richard Madeira, left, Bob Givers, right.*

QUESTIONS TO PONDER

1. The main characters in this story are TJ, Dave, and Big Bear. What makes each one of these characters special?

2. What part does the storm play in the plot?

3. How does this story knock down stereotypes that we have of bikers and the handicapped?

4. The good characters in the story are caring, compassionate people. Give some examples of how these virtues are displayed.

5. Identify the images which have stuck in your imagination. For example, the file of the bikers described as a centipede.

6. What does the eagle symbolize?

7. What have you learned about the MDA?

8. This story, we are told, is based upon real life experience and real people. How does this story read as fiction?

9. What experiences in your lifetime does this story bring to mind?

CPSIA information can be obtained
at www.ICGtesting.com
Printed in the USA
BVOW09s1945241117
501179BV00001B/278/P